Hope you had a "peary" nice time !

Dragon Wagon

Screech Beach

Grasshopper Mopper

Skunk Dunk

Sunny Bunny

Chick Kick

Gator Waiter

Smile File

Stump Bump

Sand Hand

Bug Mug

Broom Groom

Beam Team

Note Coat

Ranger Danger

Ref Chef

aer
ouy

Vowel Owl

Newborn Corn

Fox Box

Snowflake Cake

Knight Light

Book Crook

Goat Float

Nine Vine

Flower Power

Bean Queen

Sunny Money

Snow Toe

Spoon Tune

Shark Park

Ice Cream Dream

Rocket Pocket

Raccoon Spoon

Cub Sub

Dollar Collar

Duck Buck

Cub Tub

By: Kenn Vidro

COPYRIGHT 2008

"GILBERT SQUARE BOOKS"

2115 PLYMOUTH SE

GRAND RAPIDS, MI 49506

PRINTED IN THE USA

kvidro2003@yahoo.com